P9-ASC-221

Dora Goes To The Doctor

By Ellen Rosebrough
Illustrated by Bob Roper

A Random House PICTUREBACK® Book

Random House 🏠 New York

Copyright © 2013 Viacom International Inc. All rights reserved. Published in the United States by Random House Children's Books, a division of Random House, Inc., 1745 Broadway, New York, NY 10019, and in Canada by Random House of Canada Limited, Toronto. Pictureback, Random House, and the Random House colophon are registered trademarks of Random House, Inc. Nickelodeon, Dora the Explorer, and all related titles, logos, and characters are trademarks of Viacom International Inc.
randomhouse.com/kids
ISBN 978-0-449-81771-1
MANUFACTURED IN CHINA   10 9 8 7 6 5 4 3 2 1

¡**HOLa!** *Soy Dora.* Today my *mami* is taking me for a checkup at the doctor. Will you come with me? Great! *¡Vámonos!*

First we have to find the examination room. Who do we ask for help when we don't know which way to go? Yeah, Map!

Map says first we have to go to the bus stop and take the number four bus to the doctor's office. Then we go into the waiting room, where the nurse will call us into the examination room for my checkup.

Here we are at the bus stop. There are three buses coming. Do you see the number four bus? That's the one that will take us to the doctor's office. There it is! *¡Número cuatro!* Number four! *¡Vámonos!* Let's get on the bus!

The bus took us to the doctor's office. There are lots of books and toys to play with in the waiting room. In a few minutes, Dr. Lopez will be ready for me!

Nurse Pilar calls me into the examination room—it's time for my checkup! First Nurse Pilar weighs and measures me to see how much I've grown. Do you know how tall you are and how much you weigh?

Then Nurse Pilar takes my temperature by putting a thermometer in my mouth. She says my temperature is just right!

Now it's time for Dr. Lopez to come in and examine me. First she wants to listen to my heart with her stethoscope. She even lets me listen! It goes *lub-dub, lub-dub.* What does your heart sound like?

The next tool Dr. Lopez needs is a little hammer to test my reflexes. Do you see something that looks like a little hammer?

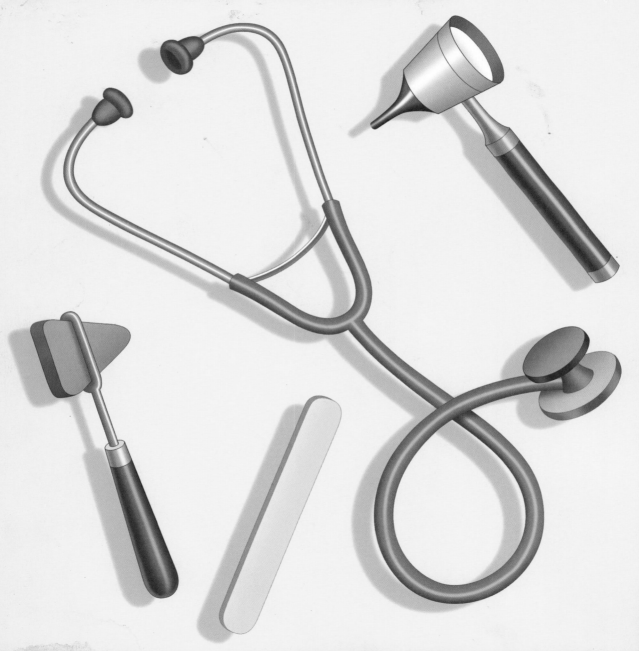

Yes, here it is! Dr. Lopez taps both my knees and makes them jump all by themselves!

Dr. Lopez asks me to open my mouth wide and make an "ahhh" sound so she can look at my throat. Will you make an "ahhh" sound with me? Say "Ahhh!"

Then Dr. Lopez takes a little stick called a tongue depressor. It looks like a Popsicle stick! She gently presses on my tongue so she can see my throat.

Her next tool is something called an otoscope. It has a little light on it to help her see into my eyes and ears and nose.

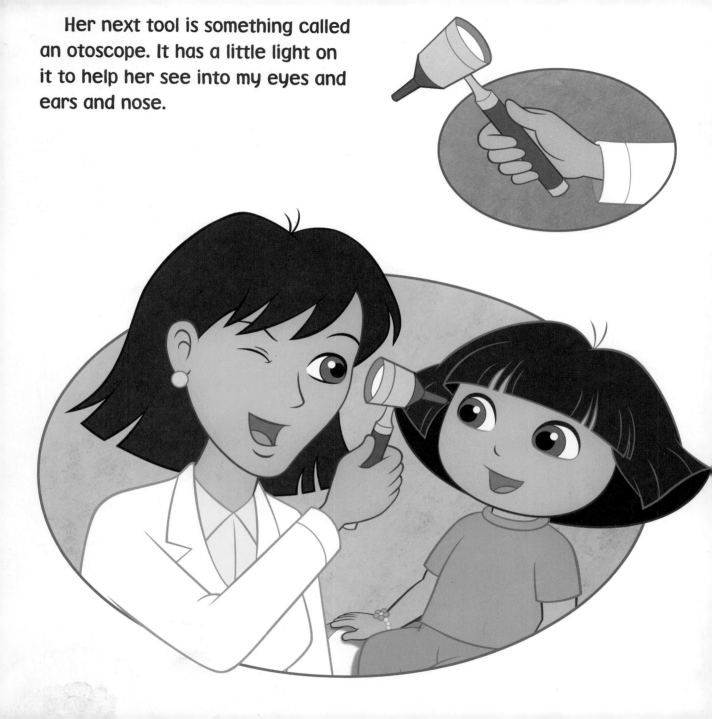

The last thing Dr. Lopez does is feel my tummy. She presses it a little bit all around. That tickles!

My checkup is over. Dr. Lopez used all sorts of interesting instruments to make sure I'm healthy. And I *am* healthy! *¡Tengo salud!*

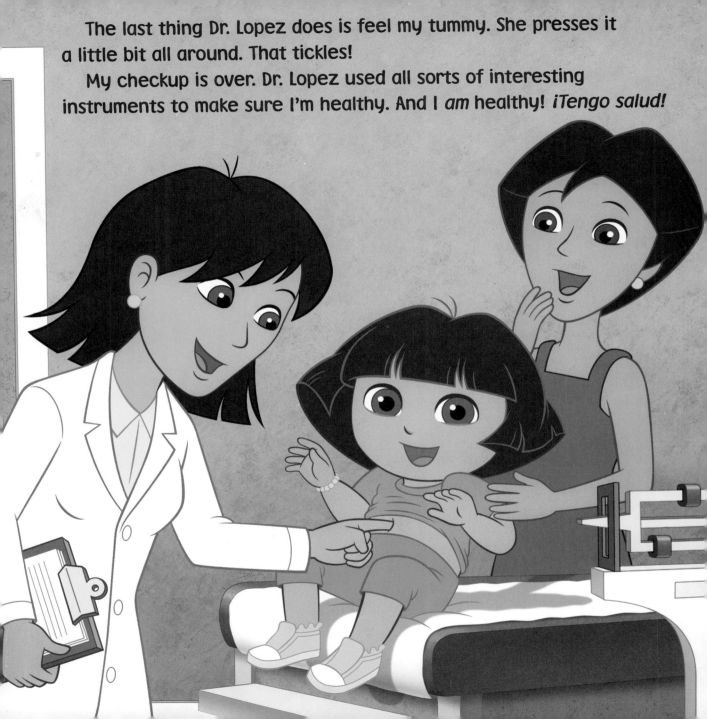

Mami says I was very brave at my checkup. She says you were, too.
I couldn't have done it without your help. *¡Gracias!*

¡Excelente! Now I have bright, clean, shiny teeth.
Going to the dentist makes me want to SMILE! Show me your smile!
Good smiling! We did it!

He uses a tool to get my tooth ready for the filling. It makes a funny whirring sound as it spins around and around. Then the dentist fills the hole. Now my tooth is better! All my teeth feel shiny and new!

The dentist checked my X-ray and found a cavity in one of my teeth. A cavity is a little hole. The dentist needs to fill the cavity so it doesn't get any bigger.

Time to floss! The dentist takes a long piece of waxy string called dental floss and wiggles it between my teeth. He says that I should have my *mami* help me floss every night to make sure the spaces between my teeth stay clean.

I need to open my mouth really wide so the dentist can check my teeth. Can you open your mouth really wide? Great! Open wide! *¡Abre!*

First the dentist cleans my teeth with a special tool. Then he shows me how to brush my teeth with a toothbrush. The dentist says I should brush after breakfast and again before bedtime.

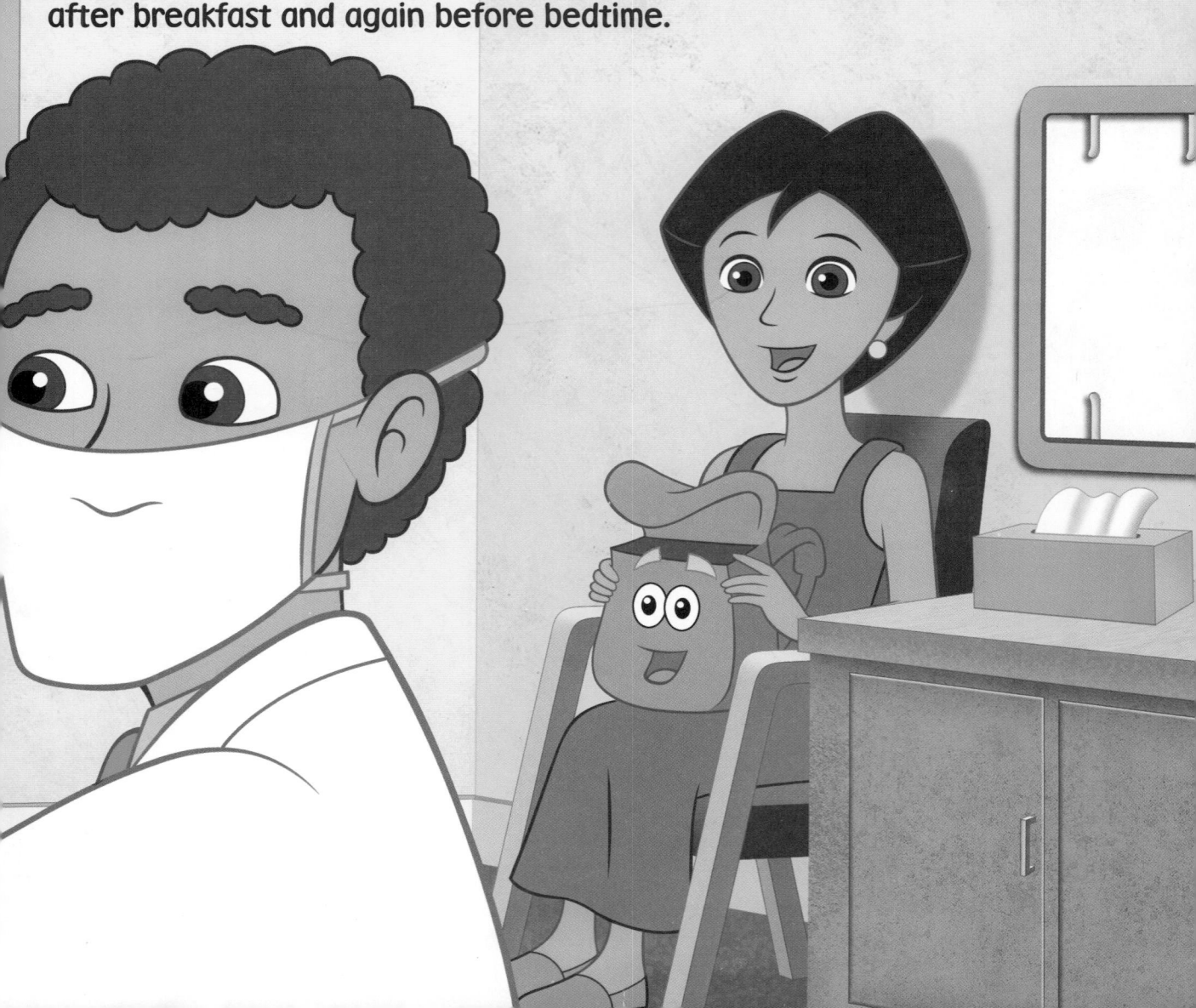

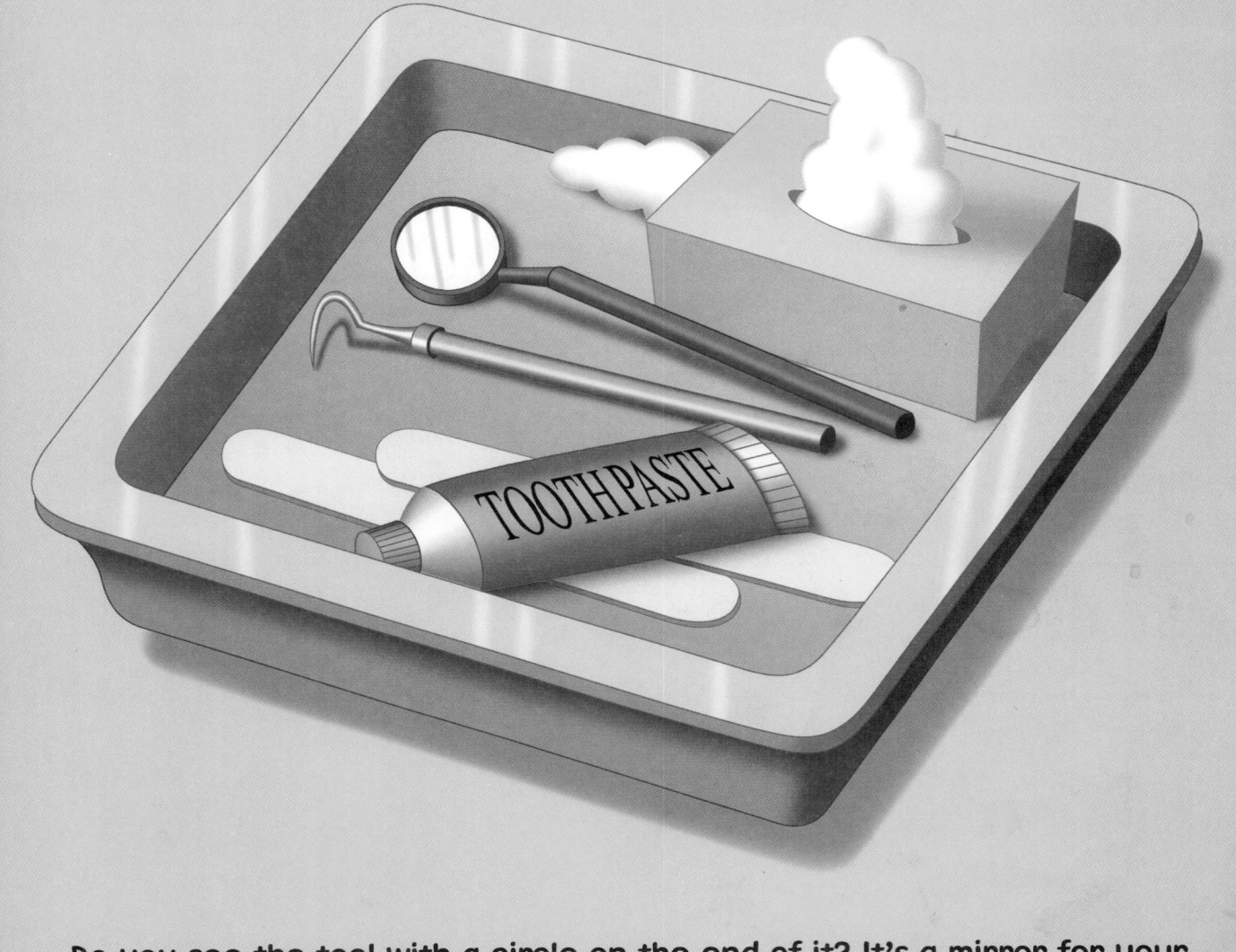

Do you see the tool with a circle on the end of it? It's a mirror for your mouth! The dentist uses it to see all the hidden areas around your teeth. The tool with a hook on the end is called an explorer. The dentist uses it to explore your teeth. Hey, the dentist is an explorer—just like me!

Here comes the dentist! He uses special tools to check and clean my teeth.

It's time for the dental assistant to X-ray my teeth. The X-ray is a picture of the bones and teeth inside my mouth. The dentist can look at it to make sure my teeth are healthy.

The dental assistant covers me with a heavy apron and takes a picture with the camera. When the camera goes *click*, the X-ray is done!

The dental assistant calls my name and we go into the dentist's office. Wow! Look at all the neat things! There's a big chair that goes up and down. Do you see a light? The dentist needs a light to see inside my mouth. What else do you see in the dentist's room?

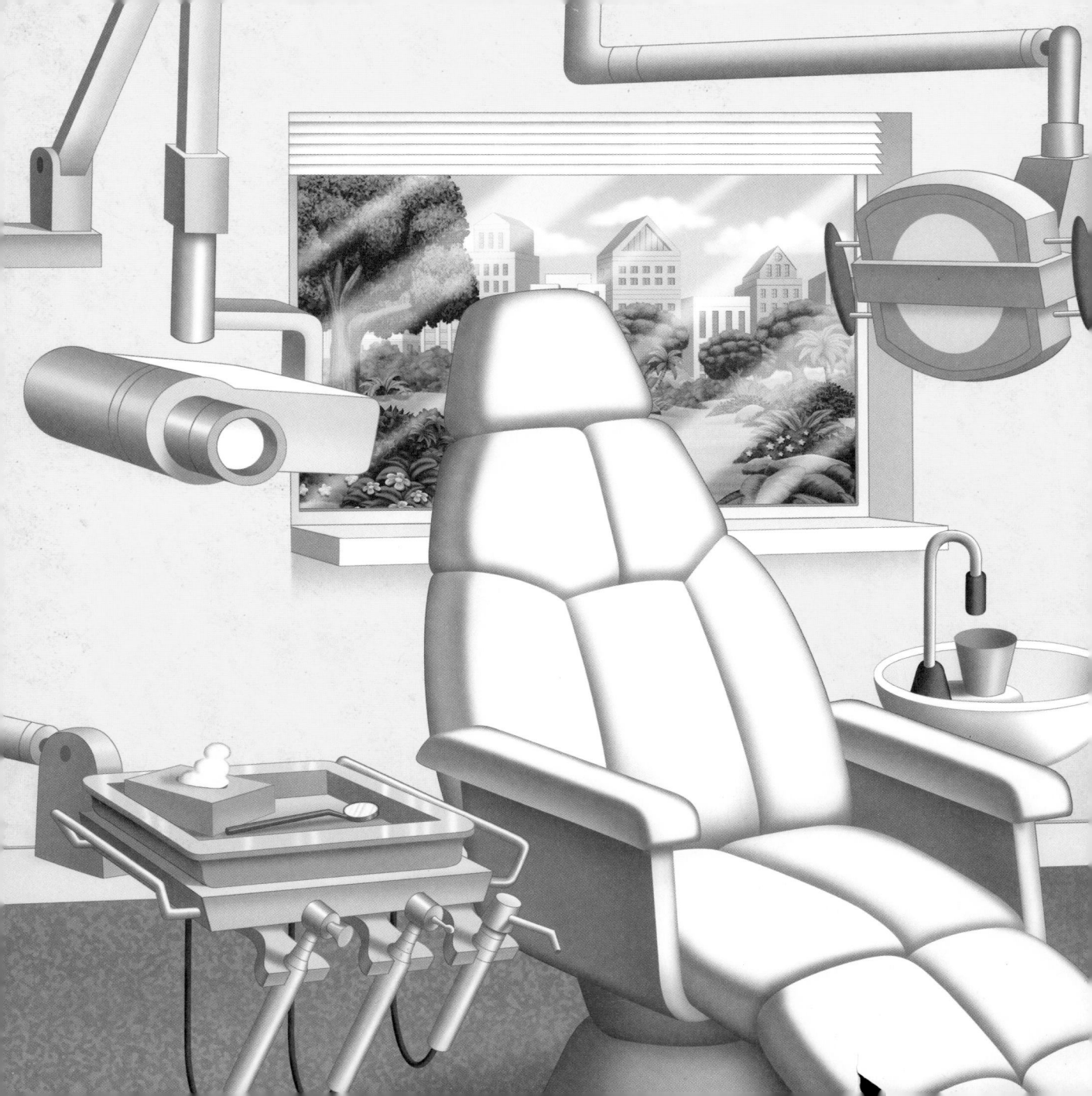

¡HoLa! *Soy Dora.* I'm at the dentist's office to have my teeth cleaned today. Have you ever been to the dentist?

I have to wait for my turn with the dentist. The waiting room has lots of things to do. I want to color a picture. Do you see some crayons?

DORA GOES TO THE DENTIST

By Ellen Rosebrough
Illustrated by Bob Roper

A Random House PICTUREBACK® Book

Random House 🏠 New York

randomhouse.com/kids
ISBN 978-0-449-81771-1
MANUFACTURED IN CHINA   10 9 8 7 6 5 4 3 2 1